WHAT THE WIND TOLD

BY BETTY BOEGEHOLD

PICTURES BY EMANUEL SCHONGUT

SCHOLASTIC INC.
New York Toronto London Auckland Sydney

Boodie (Rosemary) Kinne

in loving memory

ISBN 0-590-41140-3

12 11 10 9 8 7 6 5 4 3 2 1   7 8 9/8 0/9

Printed in the U.S.A.   08

CONTENTS

TELL ME A STORY…

Tossy was tired of being sick, of being sick and
staying in bed. She was tired of looking out
her window at all the other windows across the way.
She was tired of listening to the wind. "Stop
blowing, Wind," she said, "and tell me a story."
"All right," said the Wind, "what shall I tell you?"

Tossy thought. Then she said, "Tell me about the
windows across the way."
"Very well," said the Wind. "After all, windows are
named after me. Pick your window, and I shall tell
you a story."

Tossy looked at the windows.
"Tell me about
the old woman," she said.
"Why does she lean
on a cushion in her window
every day?"

THE OLD WOMAN'S WINDOW

The Wind said, "The old woman leans on a cushion
in her window every day for a very good reason.
She has to. For every day, exactly at ten o'clock,
her floor turns into a pond! If she didn't lean
on a cushion in her window, she would get her
feet wet.

"The old woman has some furniture of course. But it is all nailed high up on the walls. The chairs, the table, the stove, the bed. So when the floor turns to water the furniture stays dry.

"The old woman has a cat, too. He isn't nailed
to the wall like the cupboard, the TV and the
refrigerator. He sits on the table and stares into
the water, looking for fish to catch."

"Does he ever get one?" asked Tossy.

"No," said the Wind, "he never has time, because every day, at eleven o'clock exactly, the floor comes back again. The cat jumps down and walks around. But not the old woman. She keeps leaning on the cushion and looking out the window."

"Does the old woman like having a pond in her room every day?" asked Tossy.

"Oh, yes," said the Wind. "That way, she never has to wash her floor."

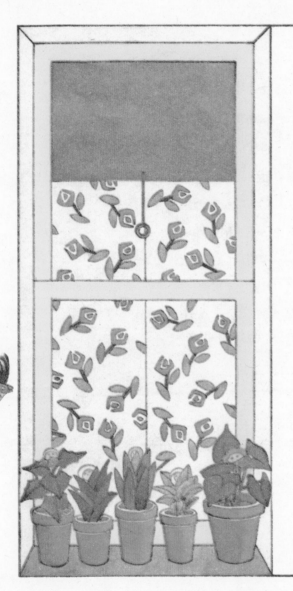

THE FIVE PLANT WINDOW

The second day, Tossy said
to the Wind, "Tell me about
the window with five plants
in it. Who lives there?"
"The Plants live there,"
said the Wind. "Only the
Plants. Mr. and Mrs. Plant,
Grandmother Plant,
Aunt Eudora Cactus
and Uncle Runner Bean.

"The five little plants in the window are their children. They put the children out in the spring and take them inside in the winter. Of course, the Plants don't have rugs. Only deep dirt on the floor with lots of worms in it, and a little puddle in the middle. There are holes in the roof, so the rain comes in. Nobody there minds a muddy floor.

"They haven't a TV of course. They listen to garden talks on the radio. Mr. and Mrs. Plant, Grandmother Plant, Aunt Eudora Cactus and Uncle Runner Bean like a quiet life."

"I'm sorry for the Plant children out on the window-sill all summer," said Tossy.

"Don't be," said the Wind. "They can stay up as late as they like."

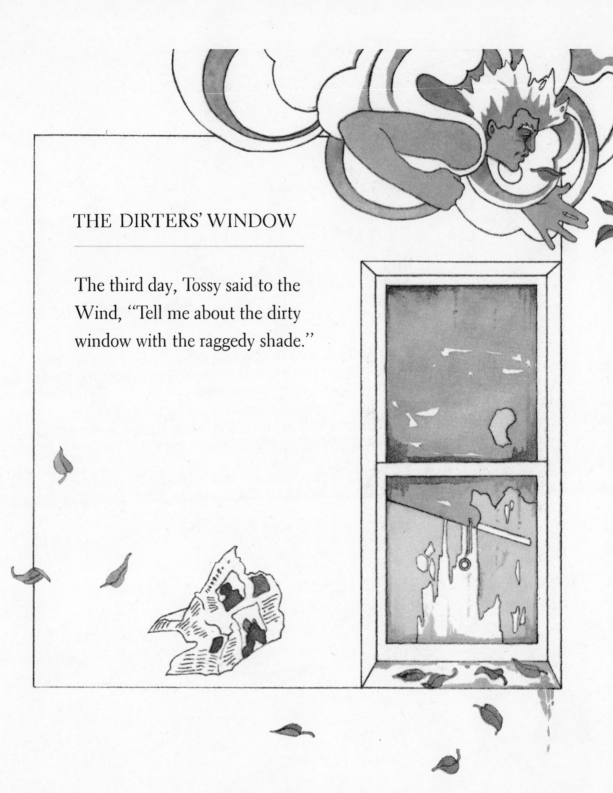

THE DIRTERS' WINDOW

The third day, Tossy said to the Wind, "Tell me about the dirty window with the raggedy shade."

"That is where the busy Dirters
live," said the Wind. "They work
very, very hard dirtying up the
city. They practice at home.
Ma Dirter tears up papers and
throws them around. Pa Dirter
squashes old cans and tosses them
everywhere. The little Dirters
smear the walls with crayons,
jelly and soup. They often
borrow mud from the Plant family.

"They make a mess of the toys and furniture and windows. Their rule is—don't hang things up, throw them down. Then every night, while everyone's asleep, the Dirters go out and dirty up the city. They are always cross and always tired because people insist on cleaning up the city the next day."

"You'd think the Dirters would be sick," said Tossy. "Living in all that dirt."

"Sometimes they are," said the Wind. "Very sick. But that's the way the Dirters like it."

THE OLD DOG'S WINDOW

The fourth day, Tossy said, "Tell me about the window where the man who looks like an old dog sits typing all day."

"He *is* an old dog," said
the Wind. "A very old dog.
And all day long he types
names. All day and all night
he is making up names for
everything.

"Names like *fire hydrant, play street, wading pool, bus stop, one way, shoe store, exit, bubble gum, police station, hot dog, pizzeria.* No wonder his paws are tired. He has nothing in his apartment but one table, one typewriter and one chair. When the old dog is hungry, he types out his favorite dinner—*chicken soup, chicken bones and gravy.* Then he eats up the words and goes back to work."

"Poor dog," said Tossy. "Doesn't he ever play?"

"Well, he's making up new game names right now," replied the Wind. "Names for games like *Red Rabbits Run*, *World Spin*, *Sea Jumpers*, *Nickity-Nack-Never-Go-Back*, and *Bibbity-Bibbity-Bounce*."

"They sound like fun," said Tossy. "Will he play them with me when I'm well?"

"Blue Heavens, child!" said the Wind. "How can he? He's got to keep working—just like a dog!"

"Doesn't he ever rest?" asked Tossy.

"Of course," answered the Wind.

"Every time he types out a comfortable word, like *chair* or *cushion*, *blanket* or *bed*, he curls up on it and goes to sleep."

THE SCARY WINDOW ·

On the fifth day, Tossy said, "Tell me about the
scary window. The one with the long heavy curtains
and the shades always down."

"It *is* a scary window," said
the Wind, "because two scared
monsters named Drool and Gool
live behind it. They are scared
of everyone and everything.
Once Drool went out for a walk
and met two children face to face.

"He was so scared he ran all the way back to the
apartment on his big flapping feet and never went
out again. That was twenty-four years ago. As for Gool,
he is even afraid to look out the window.
That is why the shade is always down.

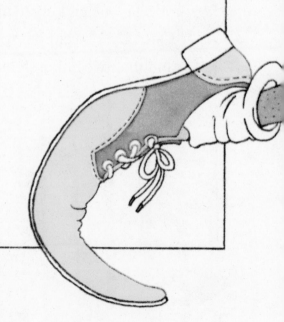

"Drool and Gool have pushed all the furniture together in the center of the room. They have made a cave for themselves in the middle. They sit in there and talk of Uncle Nil who walked into a school by mistake. He was so scared, he scared himself to pieces and had to be swept away. If anyone rings their apartment bell, Drool shouts, 'Go away!' And Gool whispers, 'There's nobody home!' They have their food left outside the door." Tossy felt sorry for Drool and Gool. "Do you think I should call them up on the phone?" she asked the Wind.

"Goodness, no!" said the Wind. "Do you want them to scare *themselves* to pieces, too?"

THE EMPTY WINDOW

The sixth day, Tossy said, "Tell me what's inside
the empty window that's always black."

"Why, Darkness, of course," said the Wind. "Didn't you know Darkness has to go someplace in the daytime? She has a lovely apartment over there, with black velvet ceilings and walls, and wall-to-wall blackness on the floor. No furniture of course, and no kitchen. Darkness doesn't eat. She just dreams.

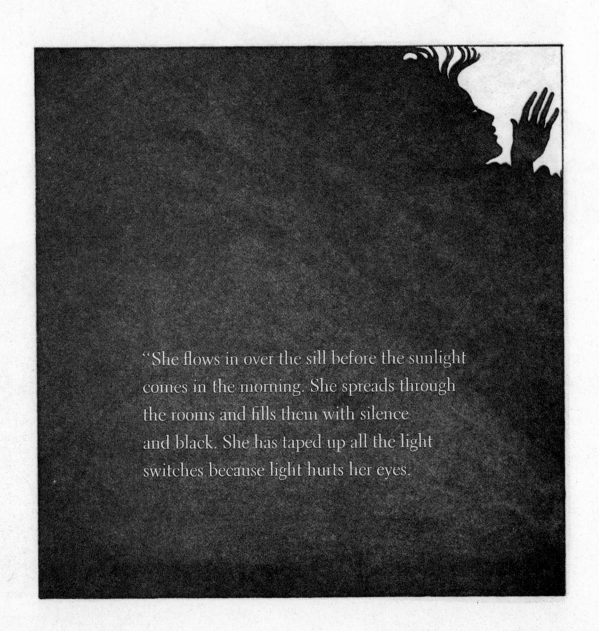

"She flows in over the sill before the sunlight comes in the morning. She spreads through the rooms and fills them with silence and black. She has taped up all the light switches because light hurts her eyes.

"Sometimes when she's bored she flips off the lights
in the whole apartment house. It amuses her to hear
people carry on about being alone in the dark.
Darkness is soft and restful. She's a very gentle lady."

"Does she have any friends?" asked Tossy.
"Everyone's her friend," said the Wind,
"when it's time to sleep."

On the seventh day, Tossy was well. The sun was shining. The sky was blue, and no wind was blowing outside her window. "Never mind," Tossy said to herself. "The wind will always blow back again and tell me more stories whenever I want to hear them."